SLIDES ON ORAL PATHOLOGY AND ORAL HISTOLOGY -

A COLOR ATLAS

Dr. R. Kalpana

CLEVER FOX PUBLISHING
Chennai, India

Published by CLEVER FOX PUBLISHING
Copyright © Dr. R. Kalpana 2023

All Rights Reserved.
ISBN: 978-93-56482-72-2

CONTENTS

Contents

ACKNOWLEDGEMENTS

First and foremost I bow in gratitude to **THE SUPREME POWER** for driving me in my performance and blessings.

I would like to express my special thanks to our respected honorable chairman **Dr.K.V Kuppusamy Ayya,** for being highly supportive and has provided the ideal academic environment to nurture the dream of authoring a textbook, without whom this project would not have been possible.

It is with a deep sense of gratitude that I would like to thank our Director **Prof Dr. Vijay V.K,** RVS Dental College and Hospital who gave me this golden opportunity and motivated me to work throughout my write up.

I would like to extend my deepest thanks to the **Principal Lt Col Dr.RGK Shet,** for his inspiration and encouragement.

I express my sincere thanks to my family members for their inspiration, encouragement and constant cooperation. I present this manual as an unassertive tribute to all their love, affection, dreams and blessings with which they have cultivated me.

I wish to acknowledge and express my gratitude to my esteemed mentor,

Dr.B.SIVAPATHASUNDHARAM, MDS, Principal,Professor and Head of the Department, Department of Oral Pathology and Oral Microbiology, Priyadharshini Dental College and Hospital, Chennai, for constant encouragement, support and relentless efforts in guiding and helping me become what I am today.

I would like to thank my friends **Dr. GIRIJA SANJAY**, **Dr.KARTHIK, Dr.SIVARAMAKRISHNAN, Dr.AMBIKA, Dr.KAVITHA** for their unconditional support and guidance.

ORAL
PATHOLOGY

DENTIGEROUS CYST

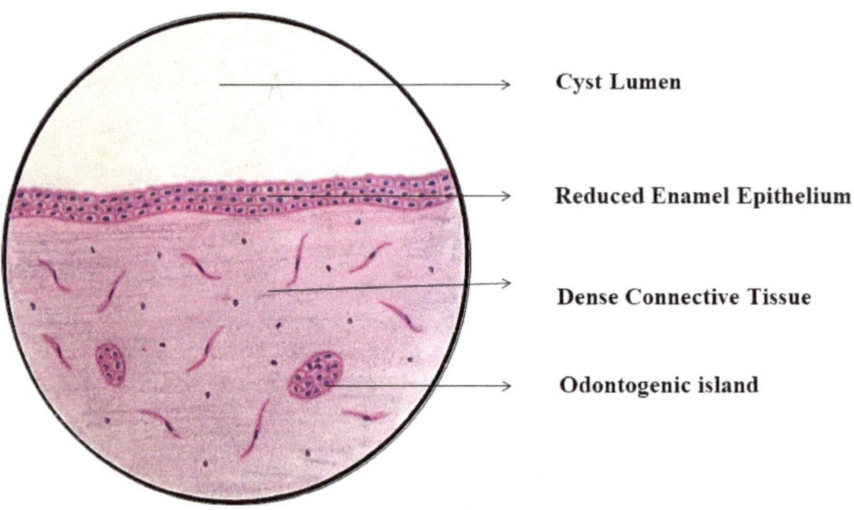

The histopathologic features of dentigerous cyst vary, depending on whether the cyst is inflamed or not inflamed.

In the noninflamed dentigerous cyst the epithelial lining consists of two to four layers of flattened non-keratinizing cells lining the lumen and the epithelium connective tissue interface is flat.

The connective tissue wall is frequently quite thickened and composed of a very loose fibrous connective tissue.

Islands of odontogenic epithelium are seen in connective tissue wall.

In inflamed dentigerous cyst presence of rushton bodies within the lining epithelium is seen.

ODONTOGENIC KERATOCYST

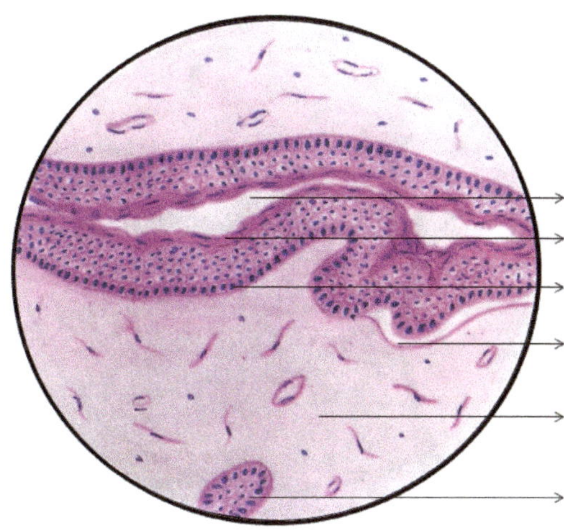

The lining epithelium is composed of parakeratinized surface which is typically corrugated, rippled or wrinkled.

Uniformity of thickness of the epithelium usually ranging from 6 to 10 cells thick

A prominent palisaded, polarized basal layer of cells often described as having a 'picket fence' or 'tombstone' appearance

The connective tissue wall often shows small islands of epithelium similar to the lining epithelium.

The apparent Islands of epithelium and small satellite or 'daughter' cyst represents the ends of folds of the lining epithelium of the main cystic cavity.

CALCIFYING ODONTOGENIC CYST

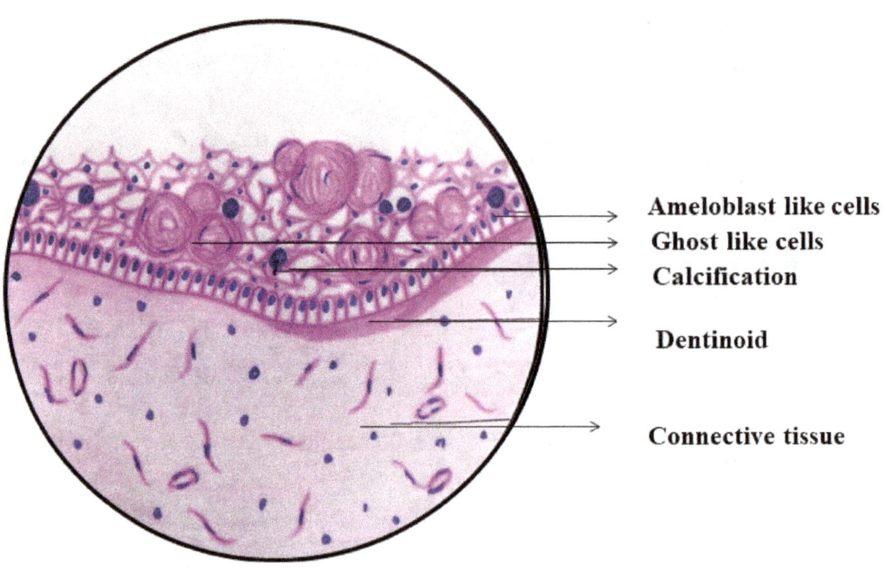

The microscopical feature of a classical COC includes a fibrous capsule with a lining of odontogenic epithelium.

The basal layer is made up of ameloblast-like columnar or cuboidal cells of 4-10 cell thickness lined by a loosely arranged epithelial cells hearing similarity to stellate reticulum of the enamel organ.

Also present are a number of epithelial cells devoid of any nuclei, which are eosinophilic with their basic cell outline retained (ghost cells).

Sometimes these ghost cells may undergo calcification and lose their cellular outline. When this happens they form firm sheet like area, of calcified keratin.

Ghost cells may be due to the effect of coagulative necrosis and dystrophic calcification or it may be a form of normal or abnormal keratinization of the odontogenic epithelium.

RADICULAR CYST

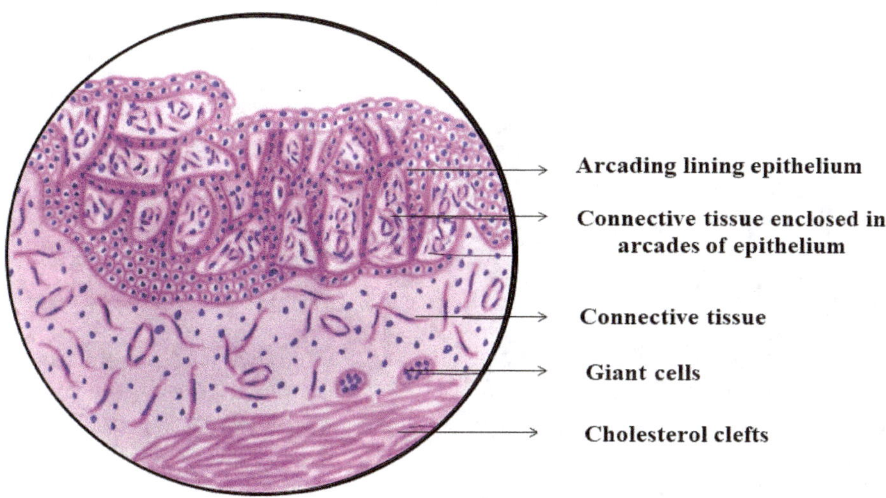

Radicular cysts are lined wholly or in part by nonkeratinized stratified squamous epithelium.

These linings may be, discontinuous in part and range in thickness from one to 50 cell layers. The majority are between six and 20 cell layers thick.

The epithelial linings may be proliferating and show arcading with an intense associated inflammatory process The inflammatory cell infiltrate in the proliferating epithelial linings consists predominantly of polymorphonuclear leucocytes whereas the adjacent fibrous capsule is infiltrated mainly by chronic inflammatory cells.

In approximately 10 per cent of periapical cysts, hyaline bodies (often referred to as Rushton's hyaline bodies) are found in the epithelial linings. Such bodies within the epithelial lining are characterized by a glassy pink (hyalinized) appearance. The origin of such bodies is believed to be related to previous hemorrhage within the inflamed cyst wall

FOLLICULAR AMELOBLASTOMA

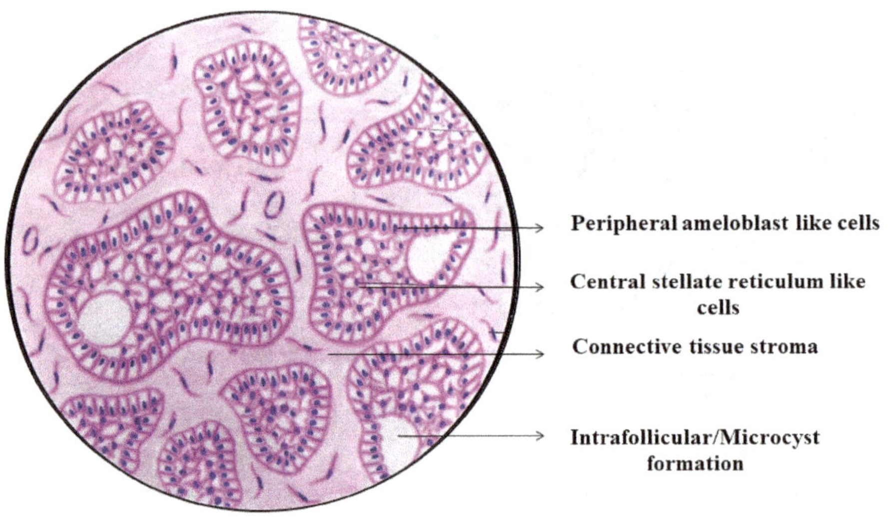

Presence of ameloblastic follicles in a fibrous connective tissue stroma

Follicular Ameloblastoma is composed of many discrete islands of tumor composed of a peripheral layer of cuboidal or columnar cells whose nuclei are generally well polarized.

These cells strongly resemble ameloblasts or preameloblasts that enclose a central mass of polyhedral, loosely arranged cells resembling the stellate reticulum.

Cyst formation is common in follicular type of ameloblastoma

In some instances, the stellate reticulum like tissue has undergone complete breakdown or cystic degeneration, and in such cases, there is often flattening of the peripheral columnar cells so that they resemble low cuboidal or even squamous cells.

PLEXIFORM AMELOBLASTOMA

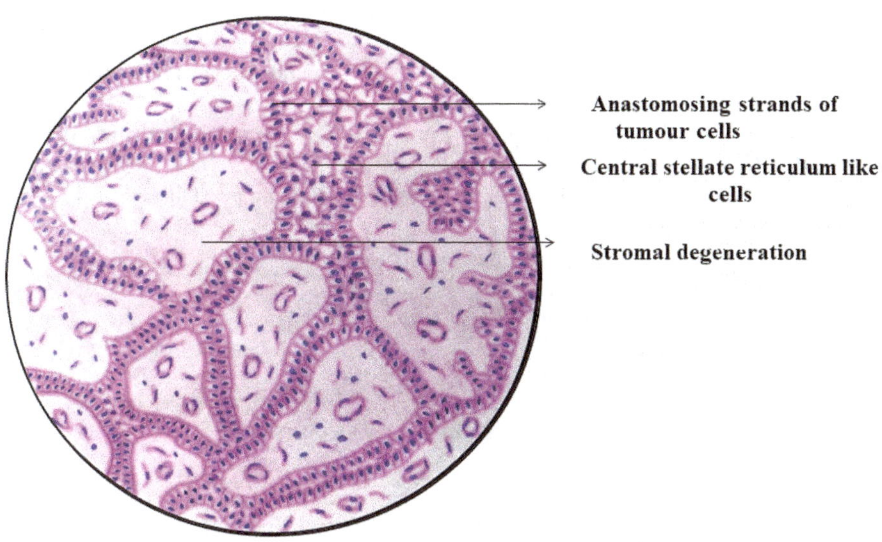

The term "plexiform" refers to the appearance of anastomosing islands of odontogenic epithelium

Plexiform ameloblastoma is composed of ameloblas like tumor cells which are arranged in irregular masses or more frequently as a network of interconnecting strands of cells.

Each of these masses or strands is bounded by a layer of columnar cells and between these layers may be found stellate reticulum like cells.

Sometimes double rows of columnar cells are lined up back to back.

The stellate reticulum like tissue is much less prominent in the plexiform type of ameloblastoma.

Areas of stromal degeneration is common.

ACANTHOMATOUS AMELOBLASTOMA

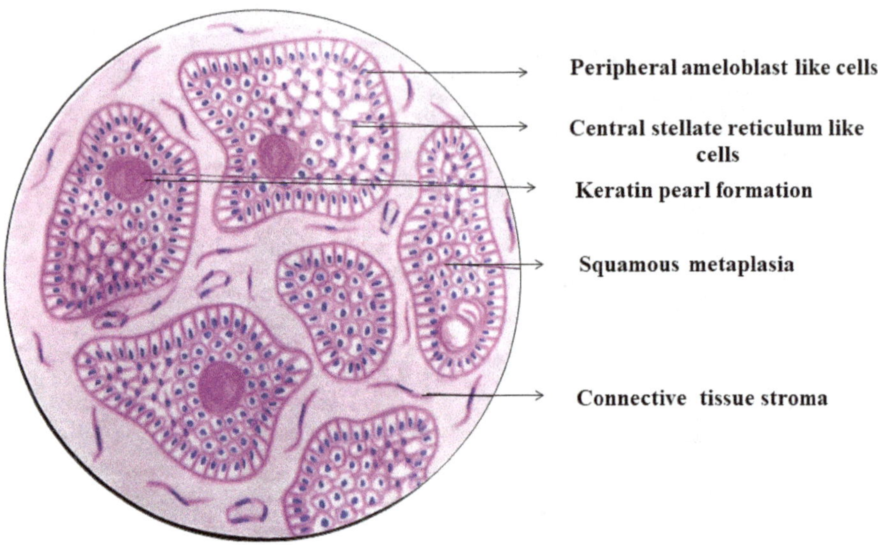

Presence of ameloblastic follicles in a fibrous connective tissue stroma

It is composed of many discrete islands of tumor composed of a peripheral layer of cuboidal or columnar cells whose nuclei are generally well polarized.

These cells strongly resemble ameloblasts or preameloblasts that encloses a central mass of polyhedral, loosely arranged cells resembling the stellate reticulum.

In acanthomatous ameloblastoma , the cells occupying the position of stellate reticulum undergo squamous metaplasia, sometimes with keratin formation in the central portion of tumor islands. This usually occurs in the follicular type of ameloblastoma

On occasion epithelial or keratin pearls may be observed.

DESMOPLASTIC AMELOBLASTOMA

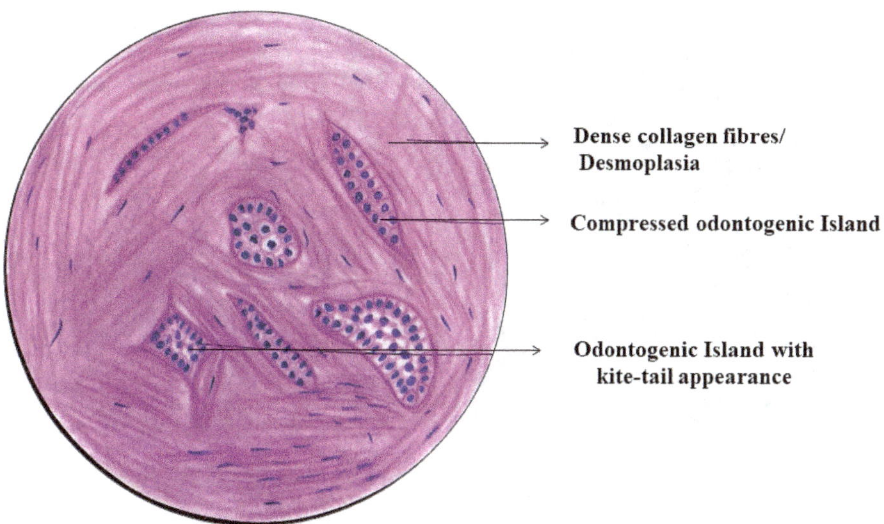

Desmoplastic ameloblastoma is found in a dense collagen stroma that may appear hyalinized and hypocellular

This has a tendency to grow in thin strands and cords of epithelium rather than in a island like pattern.

The epithelial proliferation almost seems to be compressed and fragmented by the dense hyalinized stroma

Central cells are often scant in the epithelial proliferation and the cells making up the periphery of the strands and cords often are flattened or cuboidal rather than tall columnar in appearance.

Reversal polarity of nucei and subnuclear vacuole formation may be difficult to recognize in this type of ameloblastoma

GRANULAR CELL AMELOBLASTOMA

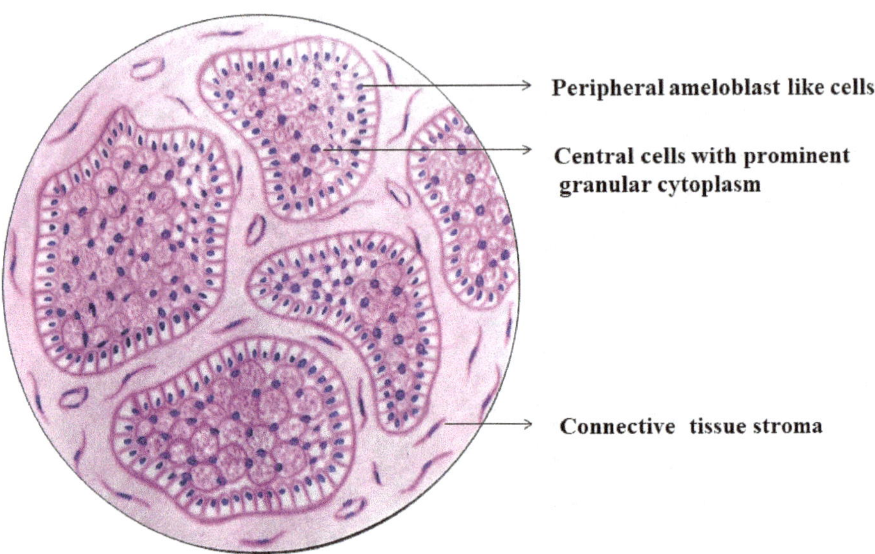

Granular cell ameloblastoma shows fibrous connective tissue exhibiting numerous odontogenic epithelial islands with peripheral tall columnar cells showing reversal of polarity.

The centre of the island shows stellate reticulum like cells. The central stellate cells may be replaced by large eosinophilic rounded or polyhedral granular cells.

The granular cells may take up a complete epithelial island and then even the basal cells are granular.

The connective tissue also shows the presence of extensive coarse granular eosinophilic cells.

The granular cells acquire small pyknotic nuclei and bulky cytoplasm filled with coarse eosinophilic granules indicating there is an apoptotic process taking place.

BASAL CELL AMELOBLASTOMA

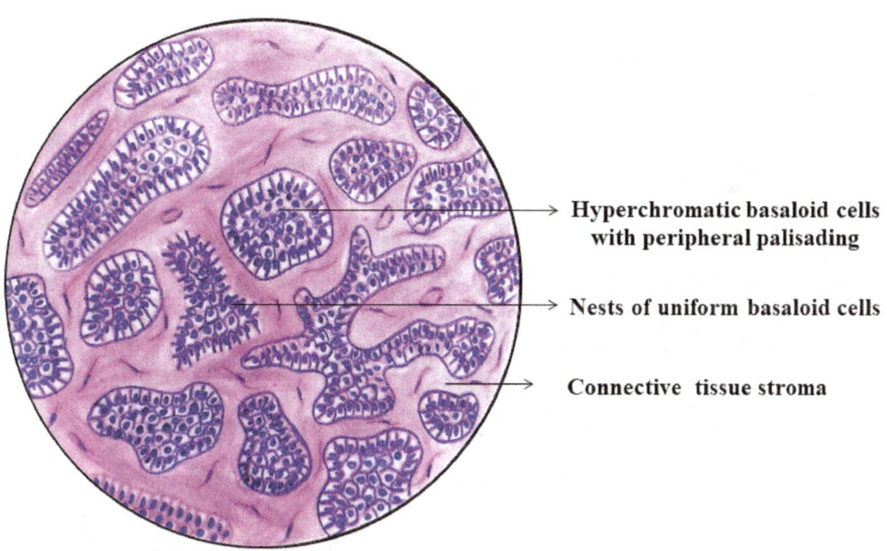

Basal cell ameloblastoma is composed of nests of uniform basaloid cells.

The peripheral cells are cuboidal to short columnar and usually do not demonstrate reverse nuclear polarity with sub-nuclear vacuole formation.

However hyperchromatism and palisading of the nuclei are retained.

The basaloid appearing cells in basal cell ameloblastoma tend to stain deeply basophilic and equivalent in staining intensity with the peripheral layer of cells.

The cells in the central portion may be polyhedral to spindle shape but stellate reticulum like areas are absent.

ADENOMATOID ODONTOGENIC TUMOUR

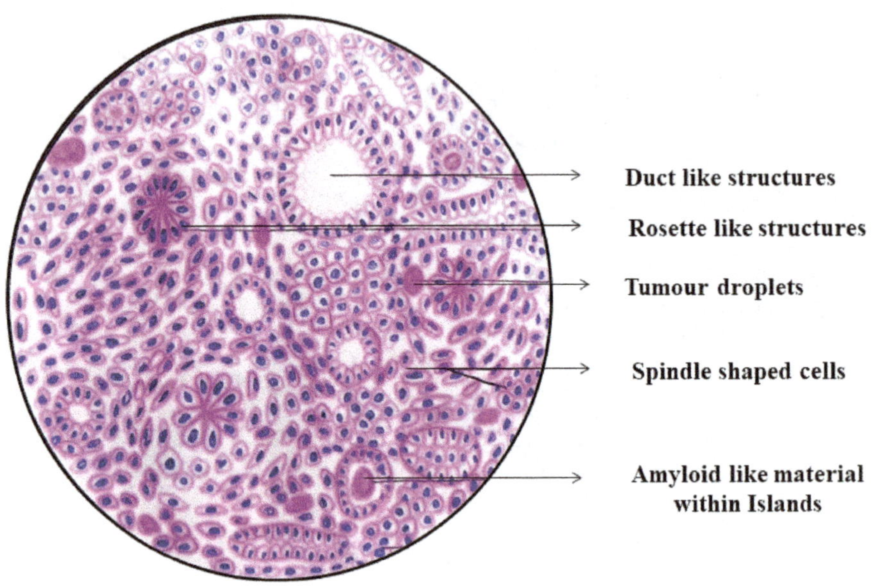

The tumor is composed of spindle shaped epithelial cells that form sheets, strands or whorled masses of cells in a scant fibrous stroma

The epithelial cells may form a rosette like structures about a central space which may be empty or contain small amounts of eosinophilic material which may stain for amyloid

The tubular or duct like structures characteristic of this tumor may be prominent, scanty or even absent. These consists of central space surrounded by a layer of columnar or cuboidal epithelial cells

The nuclei of these cells tend to be polarized away from the central space.

Small foci of calcification may also be scattered throughout the tumor. Some tumors contain large areas of matrix material which has been interpreted as dentinoid or cementum.

CALCIFYING EPITHELIAL ODONTOGENIC TUMOUR

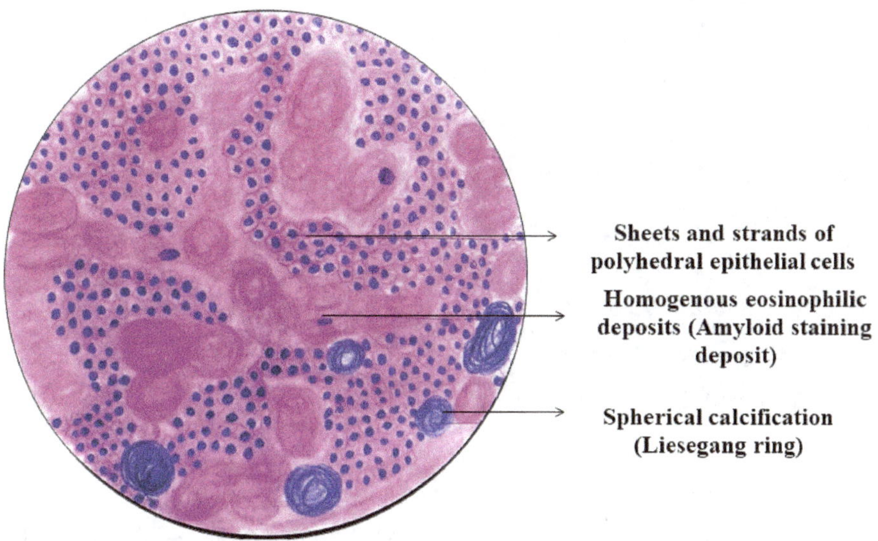

The tumor has discrete islands, strands or sheets of polyhedral epithelial cells in a fibrous stroma. The cellular outlines of the epithelial cells are distinct and intercellular bridges may be seen.

The nuclei show considerable variation and giant nuclei may be seen. Some tumors show considerable nuclear pleomorphism. Large areas of amorphous, eosinophilic hyalinized (amyloid like) extracellular material are also noted.

The tumor islands enclose masses of this hyaline material resulting in cribriform appearance.

Calcifications which are a distinctive feature of the tumor develop within the amyloid- like material and form concentric rings (Liesegang ring calcifications). These tend to fuse and form large complex masses.

AMELOBLASTIC FIBROMA

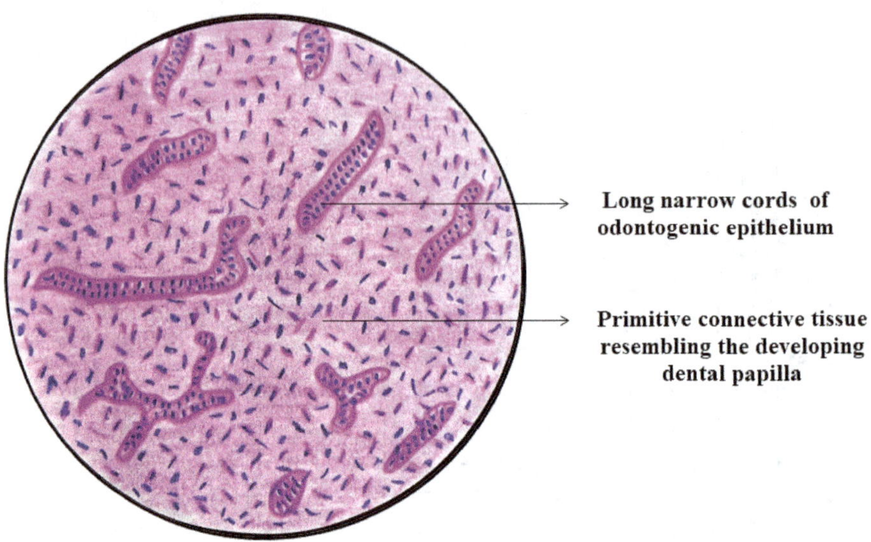

The tumour is composed of a cell-rich mesenchymal tissue resembling the primitive dental papilla admixed with proliferating odontogenic epithelium.

The most common epithelial pattern consists of long, narrow cords of odontogenic epithelium often in an anastomosing arrangement

These cords are usually only two cells in thickness and are composed of cuboidal or columnar cells

In other pattern the epithelial cells form small, discrete islands that resemble the follicular stage of the developing enamel organ with peripheral columnar cells which surround a mass of loosely arranged epithelial cells that resemble stellate reticulum

The mesenchymal portion consists of plump stellate and ovoid cells in a loose matrix which resembles the dental papilla.

COMPOUND ODONTOME

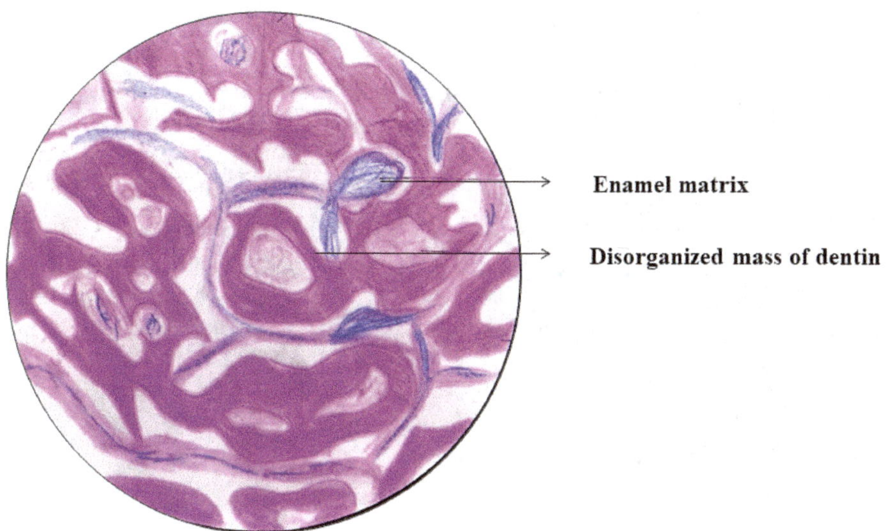

Compound odontoma consists of multiple structures resembling small, single –rooted teeth, contained in a loose fibrous matrix.

The mature enamel caps of the tooth like structures are lost during decalcification, but varying amounts of enamel matrix are often present.

Pulp tissue may be seen in the coronal and root portions of the tooth like structures.

In patients with developing odontomas, structures that resemble tooth germs are present.

PEMPHIGUS

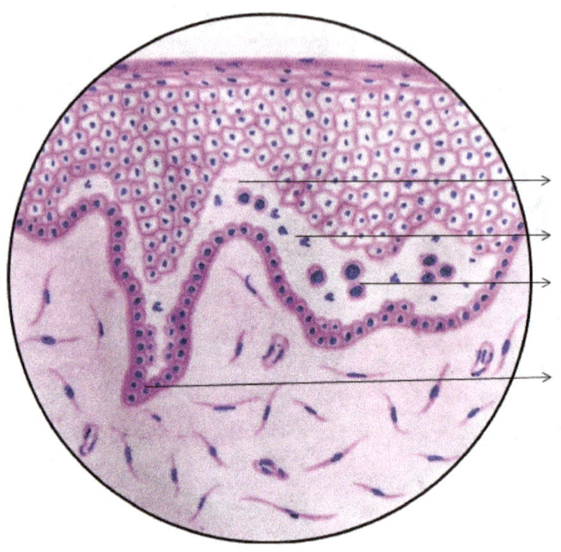

The perilesional tissue shows characteristic intraepithelial separation which occurs just above the basal layer of the epithelium

Sometimes the entire superficial layers of the epithelium are stripped away, leaving only the basal cells resembling 'row of tombstones'

The cells of the spinous layer of the surface epithelium typically appear to fall apart, termed as acantholysis and the loose cells tend to assume a rounded shape .

This feature can be used in making a diagnosis based on the identification of these rounded cells (Tzanck cells) in an exfoliative cytologic preparation

PEMPHIGOID

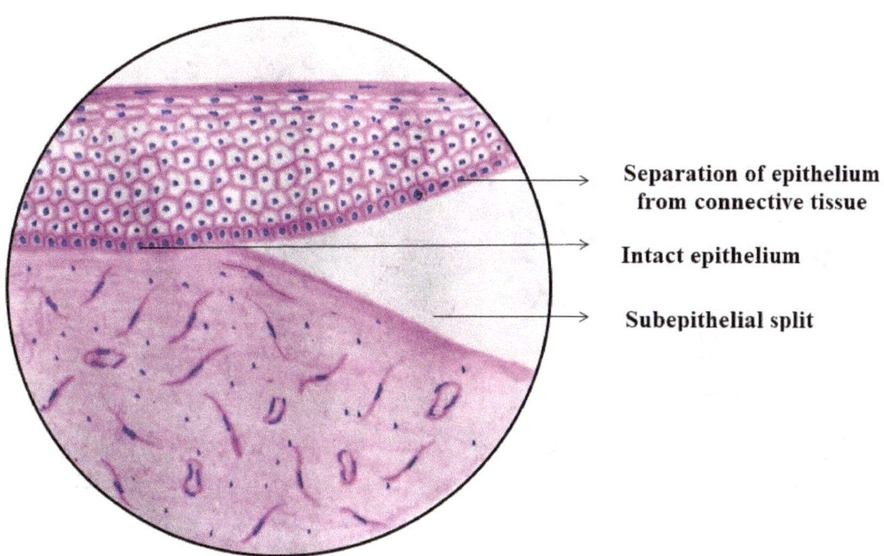

In cicatricial and bulbous pemphogoid the vesicles and bullae are subepidermal and non specific. The vesicles contains a fibrinous exudate admixed with occasional inflammatory cells.

There is no evidence of acantholysis of epithelial cells. The epithelium appears relatively normal.

In cicatricial pemphigoid the basement membrane structure appears to detach with the epithelium from the underlying connective tissue

Electron microscopy show that in contrast to cicatricial pemphigoid, the basement membrane remains attached to the connective tissue in bulbous pemphigoid.

The basement membrane also shows thickening, with interruption of continuity.

LICHEN PLANUS

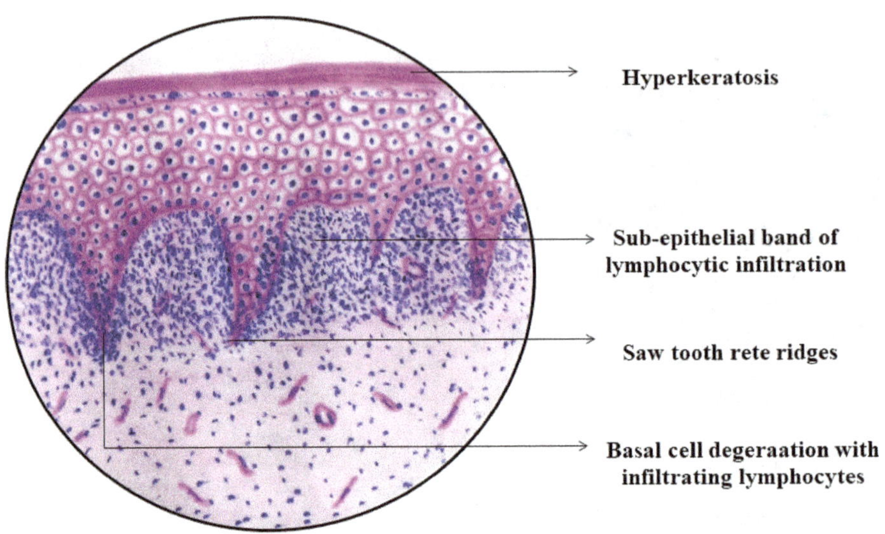

Hyperparakeratosis or hyperorthokeratosis with thickening of the granular layer, acanthosis with intracellular edema of spinous cells.

There is a destructionof basal cell by liquefaction degeneration and in some instances there is a development of saw tooth appearance of the rete pegs, due to disorganisation of the basal layer.

Band like subepithelial mononuclear infiltrate consisting of T cells and histiocytes are present, increased number of intraepithelial T Cells are also seen.

Some epithelial cells trigger the process of apoptosis and these degenerating basal keratinocyte form colloid. (civate, hyaline, cytoid) bodies, which appears as homogeneous eosinophilic gobules which are consistently seen ,at the interface between the epithelium and lamina propria

.Degeneration of the basal keratinocytes and disruption of the anchoring elements of the epithelial basement membrane and basal keratinocyte weakens the epithelial connective tissue interface.

FIBROUS DYSPLASIA

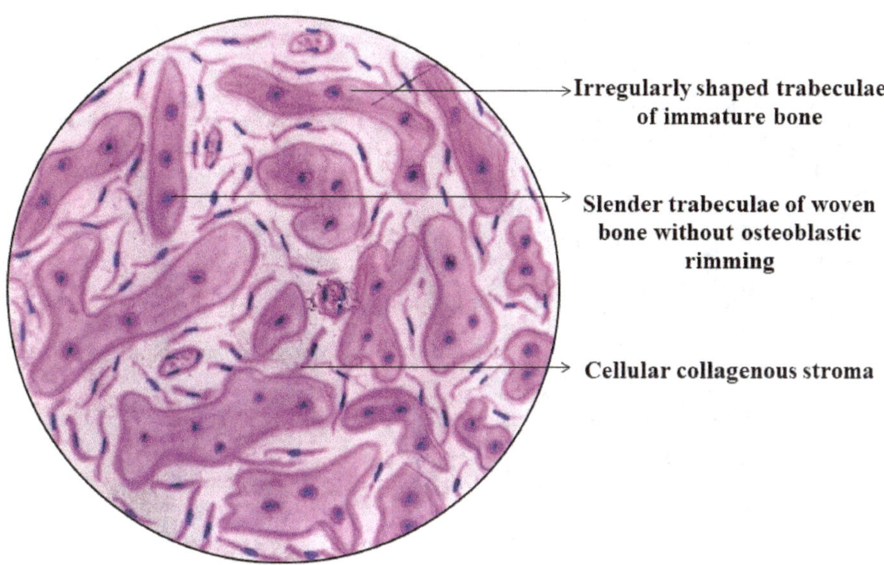

The lesion shows irregularly shaped trabeculae of immature (woven) bone in a cellular fibrous stroma.

At the periphery the lesional bone fuses with normal bone, without a capsule or line of demarcation

The abnormal bony trabeculae tend to be thin and disconnected with curvilinear shapes likened to Chinese characters

Osteoblastic rimming is usually absent or minimal and peritrabecular clefting (artifactual retraction of the stroma from the bony trabeculae)

In early stages the woven bone is replaced by lamellar bone with roughly parallel trabeculae

PAGETS DISEASE

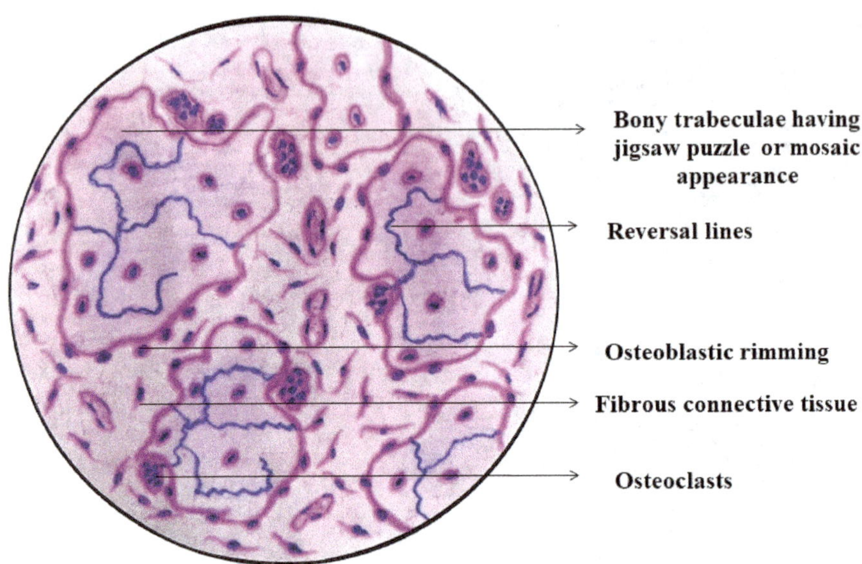

The lesion shows uncontrolled resorption and formation of bone. In the resorptive phase numerous hyperactive osteoclasts surround the bony trabeculae. These osteoclasts tend to be enlarged with an increased number of nuclei.

Highly vascular fibrous connective tissue replaces the marrow.

The osteoblasts form osteoid rims around the bone trabeculae and the bone lacks an organized lamellar pattern.

Basophilic reversal lines which indicate the junction between alternating bone resorption and formation, result in a characteristic 'jigsaw puzzle' or 'mosaic' appearance.

In the sclerotic phase there are large masses of dense bone with prominent reversal lines.

MUCOCELE

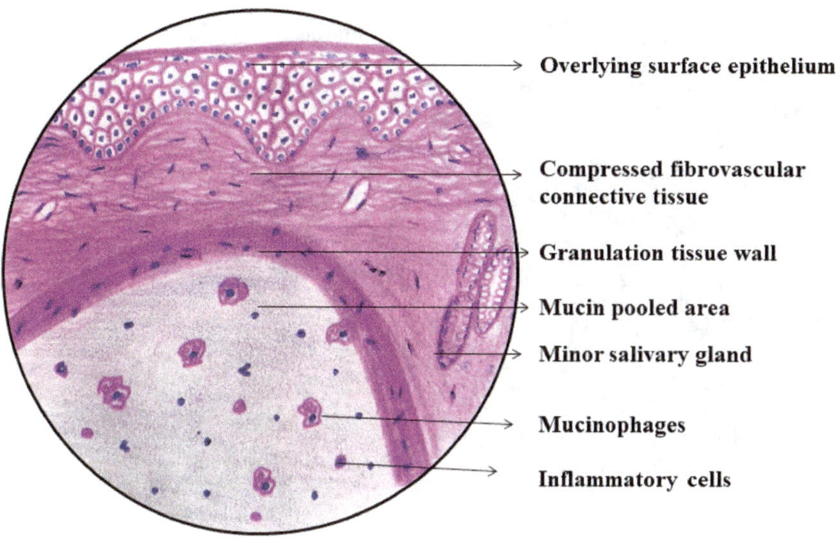

The lesion shows a central irregular mucin spilled area surrounded by a granulation tissue wall.

Extravasation of free mucin incites an inflammatory response that is followed by connective tissue repair.

Granulation tissue comprises of delicate collagen bundles, plump fibroblasts, proliferating endothelial cells, bunding capillaries and chronic inflammatory cells.

Mucinophages or mucin engulfed macrophages are seen in mucin pooled area

The adjacent salivary gland whose duct was transected shows ductal dilation, chronic inflammation, acinar degeneration and intestinal fibrosis

PLEOMORPHIC ADENOMA

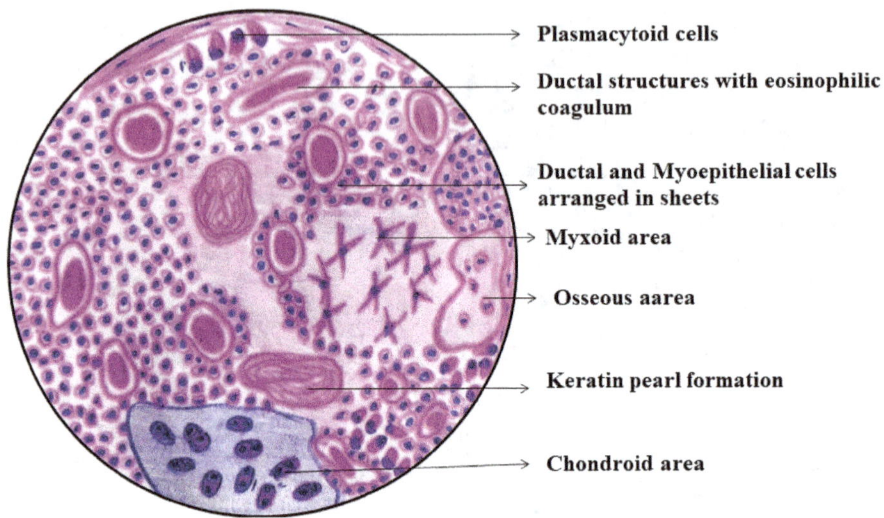

Microscopically, mixed tumors demonstrate a widw spectrum of histologic features.

The pleomorphic patterns and variable ratios of ductal to myoepithelial cells are responsible for the synonym pleomorphic adenoma

The epithelial component may appear as ducts, tubules, ribbons and solid sheets

The mesenchymal component may appear as myxoid, hyalinized connective tissue.

Myoepithelial cells may appear as plasmacytoid cells or spindled cells

The pseudocapsule surrounding mixed tumors may demonstrate islands of tissue within it or extending through it.

WARTHIN'S TUMOUR

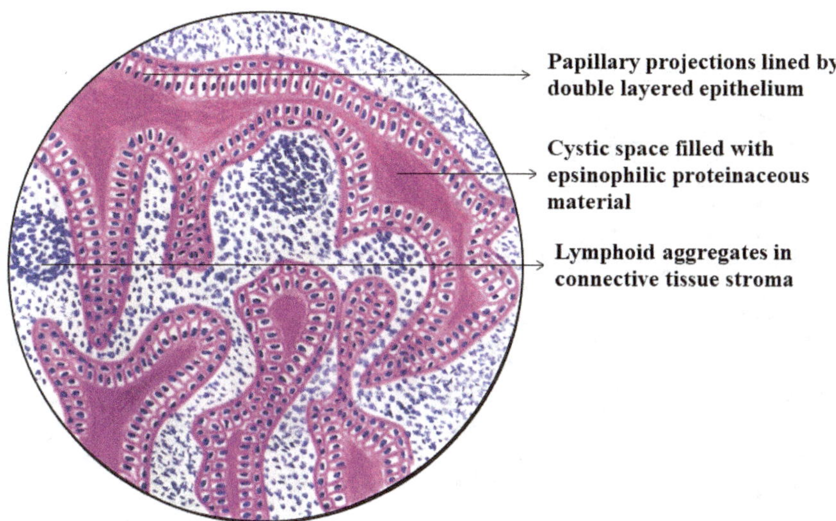

Microscopically two components are seen in warthin's tumor, epithelial and lymphoid.

This lesion is basically cystic with papillary processes lined by epithelium projecting into the cystic space.

Connective tissue has abundant lumphoid component exhibing germinal center.

Epithelium lining the papillary projections is bilayered with inner cuboidal cells and outer columnar cells

Columnar cells are regularly arranged having palisading arrangement of nuclei

Cystic space may contain eosinophilic material.

MUCOEPIDERMOID CARCINOMA

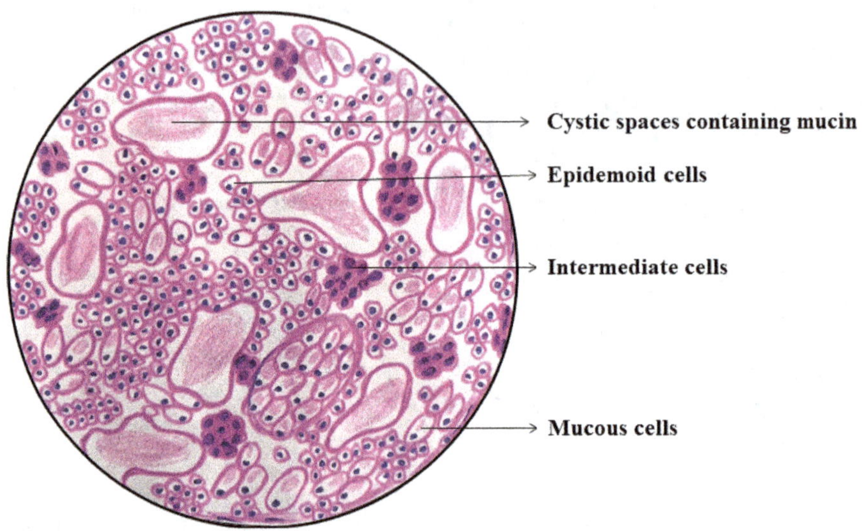

It is composed of three types of cells mucous secreting cells, epidermoid cells, intermediate cells

Epidermoid cells have squamoid features which demonstrate a polygonal shape intercellular bridges and rarely keratinisation.

The mucous cells have abundant, pale, foamy cytoplasm that stains positively for mucin stains.

Basaloid cells are larger than basal cells and smaller than the squamous cells. These are referred to as intermediate cells.

Epidermoid cells together with intermediate and mucous cells line cystic spaces or form solid masses or cords.

Epidermoid and mucous cells may be arranged in a glandular pattern.

ADENOID CYSTIC CARCINOMA

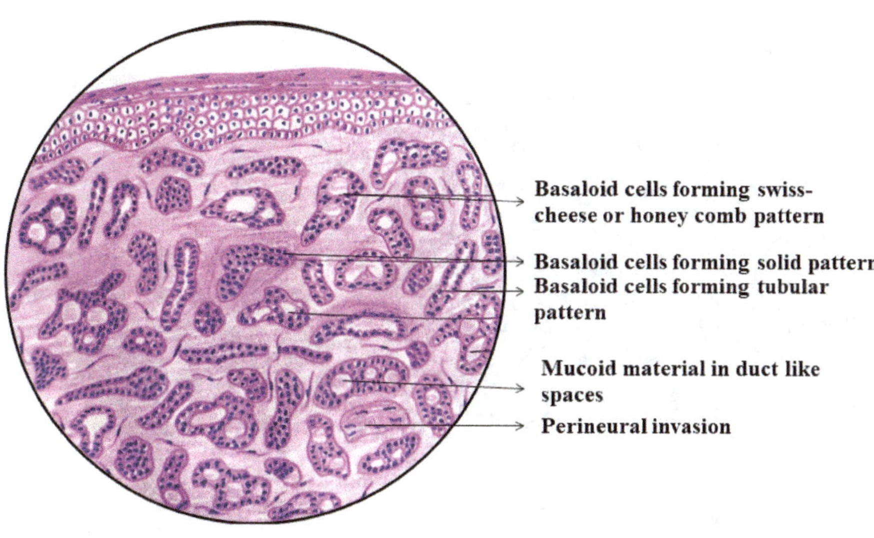

The tumor is composed of uniform cells, resembling basal cells arranged in anastomosing cords or duct like pattern.

Some of these duct like areas contain a mucoid material. The above mentioned feature gives rise to the characteristic appearance described as cribriform, 'honey comb' or 'Swiss cheese' pattern.

There may be areas where the cells show a tubular or more solid pattern.

The connective tissue component is often hyalinized, and surrounding the tumor cells, forming a structural pattern of cylinders.

The term cylindroma is given because of this cylindrical pattern

POLYMORPHOUS LOW GRADE ADENOCARCINOMA

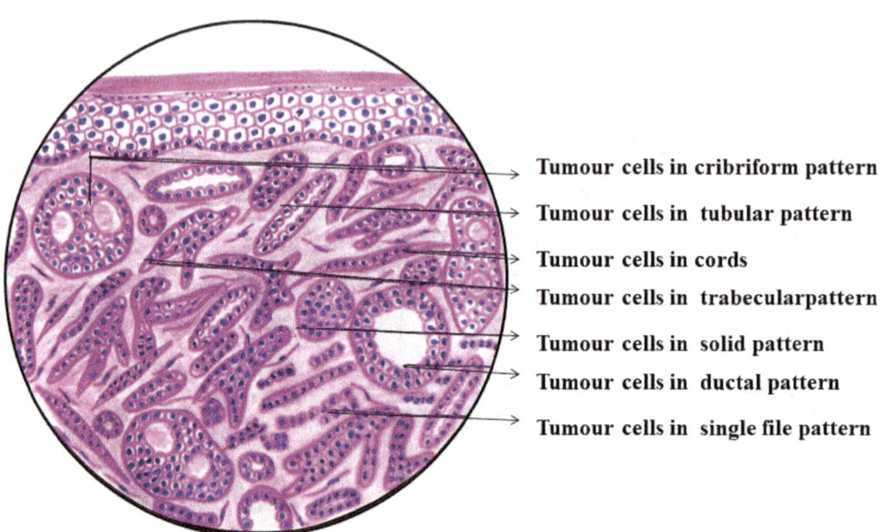

The tumor stroma consist of both mucoid and hyaline areas.

Tumor cells are arranged in various morphological patterns, such as solid, cribriform, duct-like and tubular patterns indicating morphodiversity separated by fibrovascular stroma

The tumor cells are round to oval in shape with indistinct cell borders. The cytoplasm is scanty with round, oval or spindle shaped vesiculated nuclei

At the tumor periphery, cells may be arranged in a linear, single cell arrangement resembling "Indian file" or "beads on a string" pattern of infiltration

Perineural invasion can be noted.

EPITHELIAL DYSPLASIA–MILD

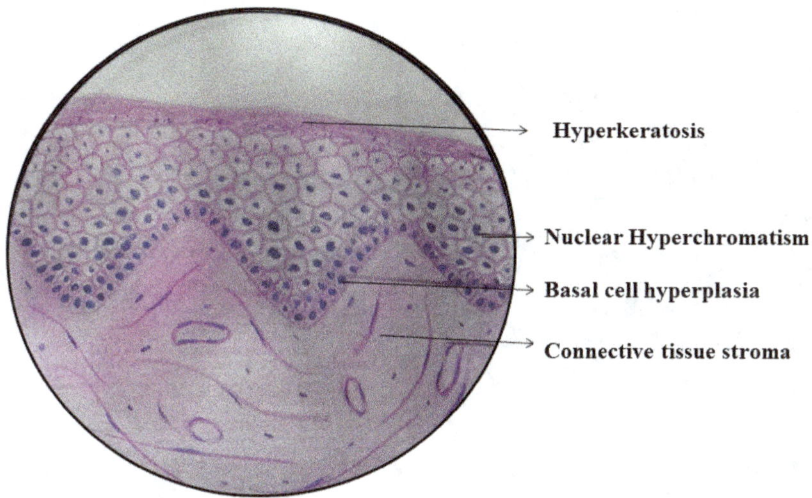

Mild epithelial dysplasia refers to alterations limited to the basal and parabasal layers.

EPITHELIAL DYSPLASIA– MODERATE

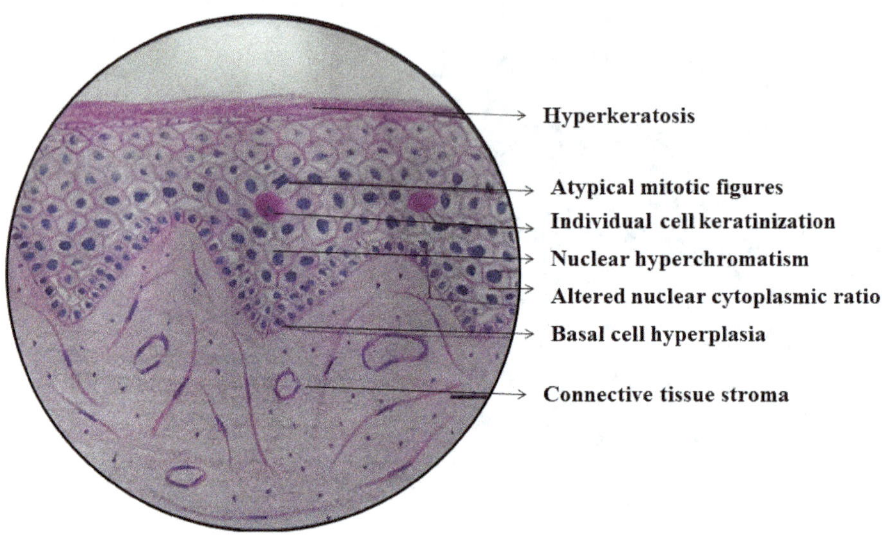

Moderate epithelial dysplasia demonstrates involvement from the basal layer to the midportion of the spinous layer

EPITHELIAL DYSPLASIA– SEVERE

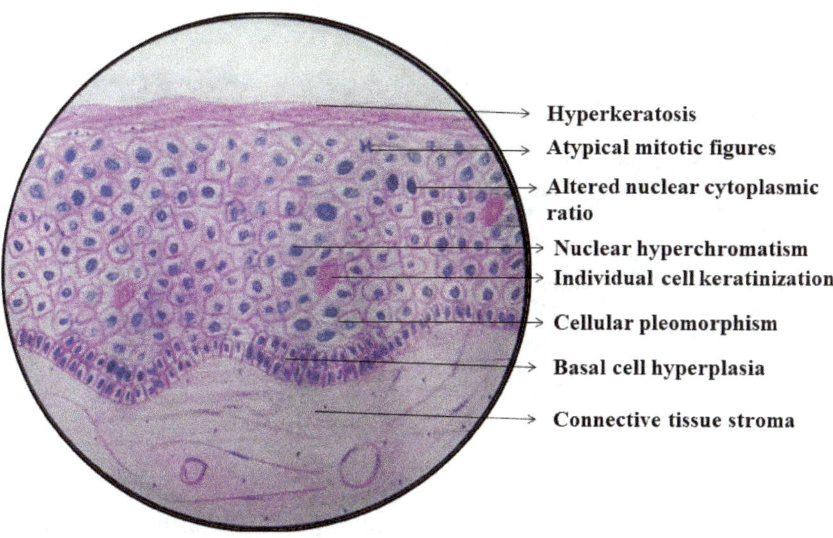

Severe epithelial dysplasia demonstrates alterations from the basal layer to a level above the midpoint of the epithelium.

Sometimes dysplasia may extend down the duct of a minor salivary gland especially in lesions of the floor of the mouth.

CARCINOMA IN SITU

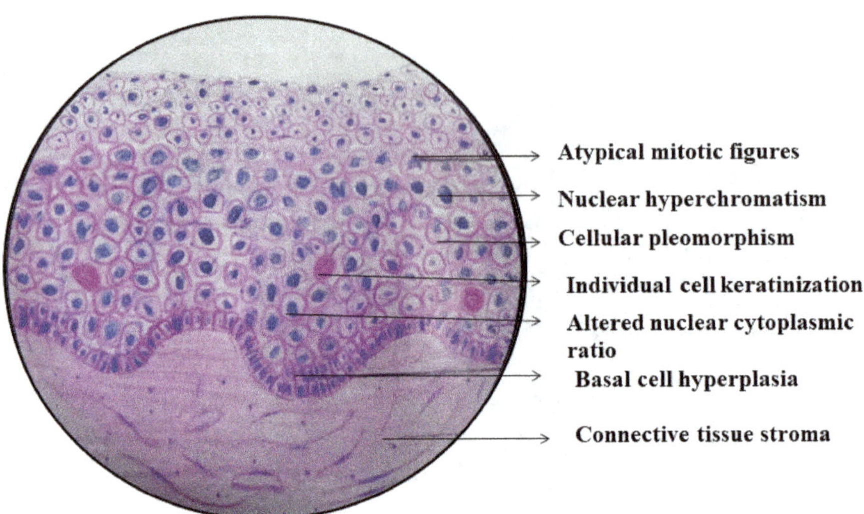

Carcinoma in situ is defined as dysplasia involving the entire thickness of the epithelium (i.e extending from the basal layer to the surface or 'top-to-bottom' change)

The epithelium may be hyperplastic or atrophic.

WELL DIFFERENTIATED SQUAMOUS CELL CARCINOMA

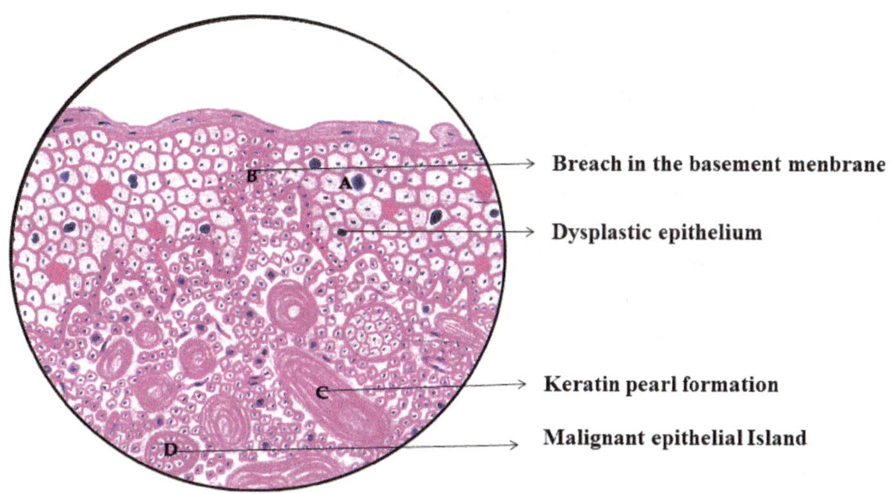

Squamous cell carcinoma arises from dysplastic surface epithelium and is characterized histopathologically by invasive islands or cords of malignant squamous epithelial cells.

Invasion is represented by irregular extension of lesional epithelium through the basement membrane and into the sub epithelial connective tissue.

Individual squamous cells and sheets or islands of cells proliferate within the connective tissue.

The lesional cells generally show increased nuclear-to-cytoplasmic ratio, hyperchromatism, varying degrees of cellular and nuclear pleomorphism and keratin pearl formation.

Histopathologic grading is based upon the degree of resemblance to normal squaamous epithelium and the amount of keratin production.

MALIGNANT MELANOMA

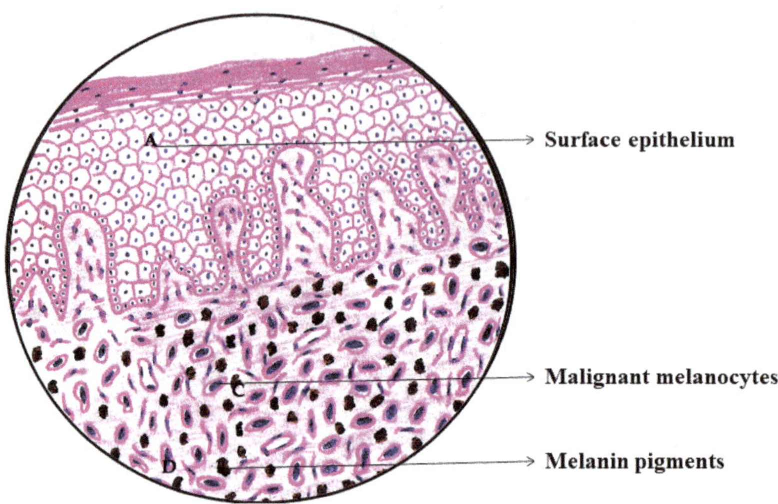

In early stages of malignant melanoma, atypical melanocytes are seen either scattered singly among the basal epithelial cells or as nests within the basal cell layer.

The atypical melanocytes are enlarged with varying degrees of nuclear pleomorphism and hyperchromatism.

The tumour usually appears as pleomorphic, spindle shaped or epithelioid cells arranged in loosely aggregated cords or sheets.

In superficial spreading melanoma, there is often pagetoid spread (i.e single tumour cells infiltrating into the upper layers of the surface epithelium. The microscopic pattern resembles an intraepithelial adenocarcinoma known as paget's disease of skin.

The spread of the lesional cells along the basal layer of the surface epithelium constitutes the radial growth phase. The vertical growth phase is characterized by malignant melanocytes invading the connective tissue.

ORAL

HISTOLOGY

BUD STAGE

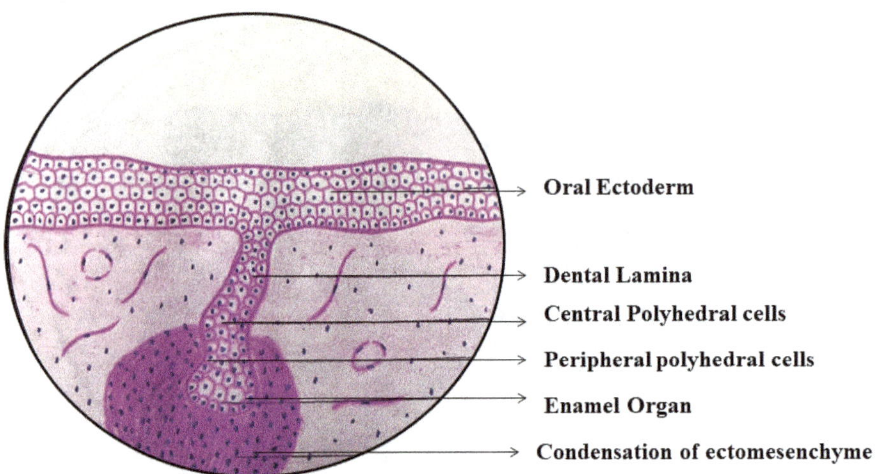

In bud stage, the enamel organ consists of peripherally located low columnar cells and centrally located polygonal cells and the enamel organ is bud shaped.

Many cells of the tooth bud and the surrounding mesenchyme undergo mitosis. As a result of the increased mitotic activity and the migration of neural crest cells into the area the ectomesenchymal cells surrounding the tooth bud condense.

The area of ectomesenchymal condensation immediately subjacent to the enamel organ is the dental papilla.

The condensed ectomesenchyme that surrounds the tooth bud and the dental papilla is the dental sac.

Both the dental papilla and dental sac become more well defined as the enamel organ grows into the cap and bell stages.

CAP STAGE

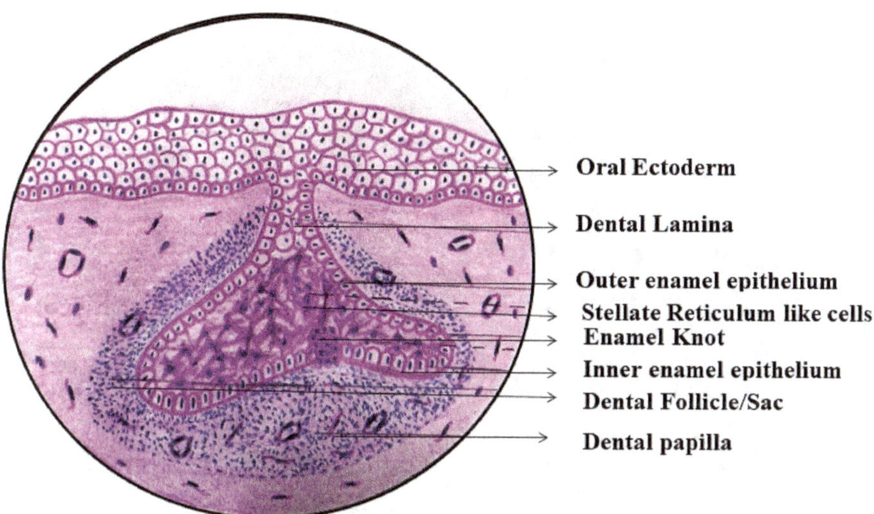

As the tooth bud continues to proliferate, it doesn't expand uniformly into a larger sphere. Instead, unequal growth in different parts of the tooth bud leads to the cap stage, which is characterized by a shallow invagination on the deep surface of the bud.

The peripheral cells of the cap stage are cuboidal, cover the convexity of the 'cap' and called the outer enamel epithelium, the cells in the concavity of the cap become tall columnar cells and called inner enamel epithelium.

Polygonal cells become star shaped but maintain contact with each other by their cytoplasmic process and forms cellular network called stellate reticulum.

The ectomesenchyme proliferates and condenses to form dental papilla, which is the formative organ of the dentin and primordium of the pulp, it shows active budding of capillaries and mitotic figures.

There is a marginal condensation in the ectomesenchyme surrounding the enamel organ and dental papilla, gradually in this zone, a denser and more fibrous layer develops, which is the primitive dental sac.

EARLY BELL STAGE

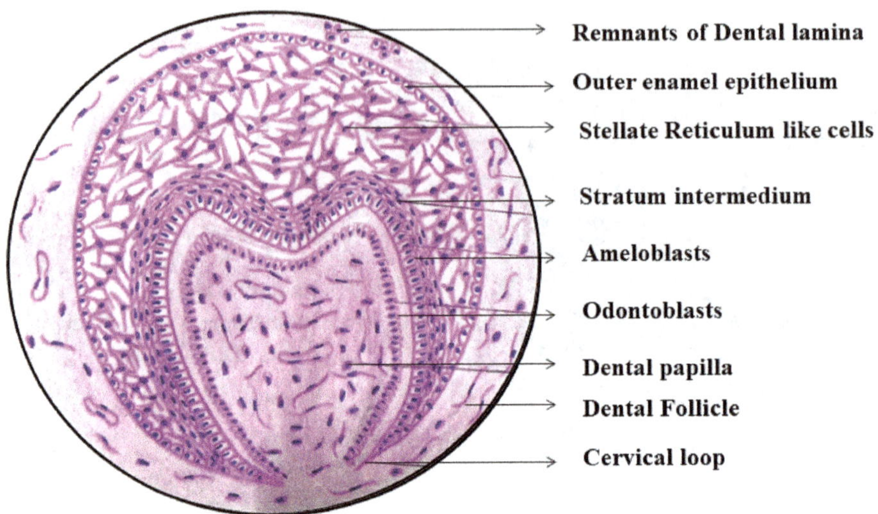

During this stage the enamel organ enlarges and the invagination deepens further to resemble a bell. Four layers in enamel organ- inner enamel epithelium, stratum intermedium, stellate reticulum, outer enamel epithelium

The inner enamel epithelial cells undergo histodifferentiation to form ameloblasts; the cells that synthesize enamel. These cells are separated from dental papilla by a distinct basementmembrane, which is called membrana preformativa

As the tooth development progresses the stellate reticulum collapses and reduce the distance between inner enamel epithelial cells and nutrient capillaries located in dental follicle adjacent to outer enamel epithelium. This is of importance as the source of nutritional supply changes after the initiation of apposition.

The dental papilla has peripheral cell differentiating to odontoblast. It has distinct dental follicle

Dental follicle has three layers: inner cellular, outer fibrous, middle loose connective tissue

ADVANCED BELL STAGE

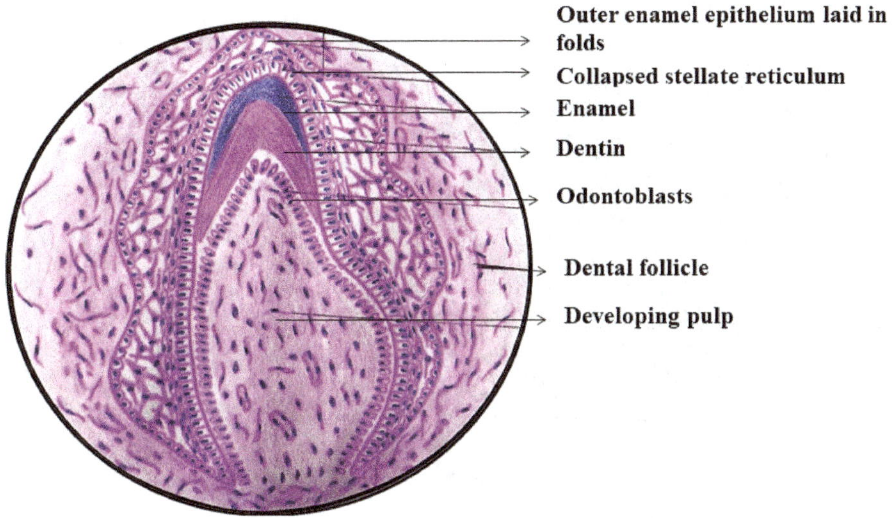

Once the apposition process begins, the tooth germ enters into advanced bell stage. Dentin is the first hard tissue formed in a tooth and enamel formation can be initiated only after a layer of dentin is deposited

As the hard tissue formation continues the outer enamel epithelium becomes more irregular and stellate reticulum collapses further.

Once the enamel and dentin formation reaches the cervical region of tooth, root formation begins by formation of Hertwig's epithelial root sheath from the cervical loop of enamel organ.

Once the formation of enamel is completed the columnar ameloblasts shorten to cuboidal and along with other collapsed layers of enamel organ form a 2-3 layered stratified epithelium which is termed as reduced enamel epithelium.s

CROSS SECTION OF ENAMEL RODS

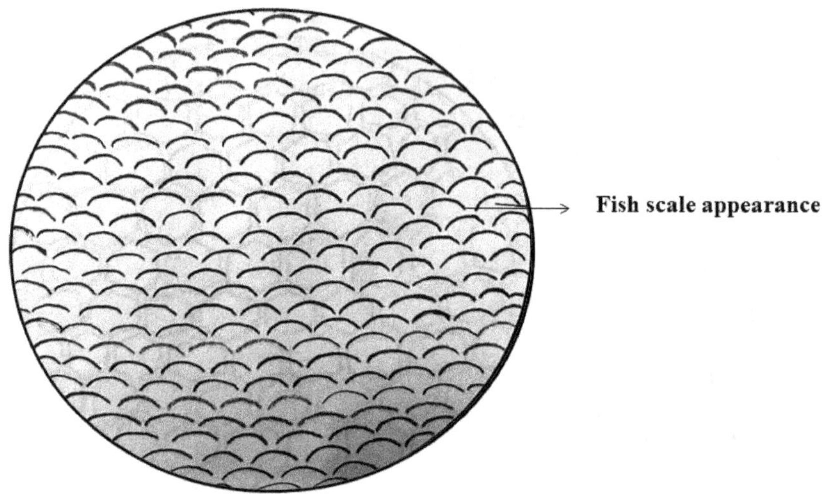

The enamel rods normally have a clear crystalline appearance, permitting light to pass through them.

In cross sections of human enamel, many rods resemble fish scales.

CROSS SECTION OF ENAMEL RODS

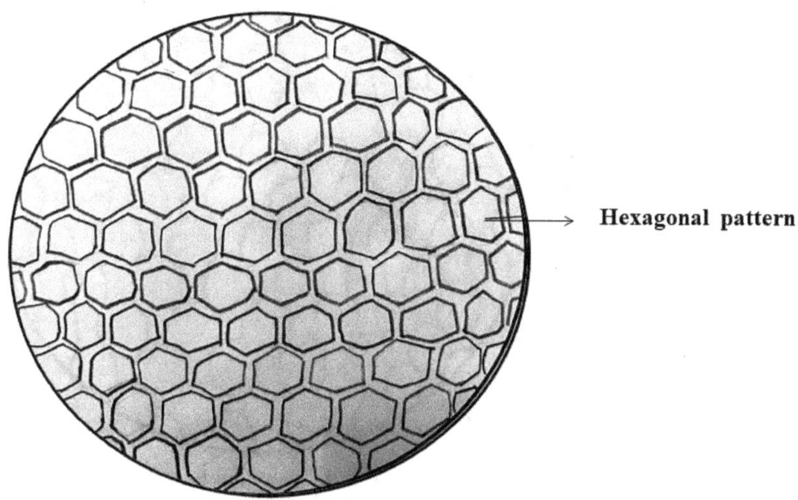

In cross- section under the light microscope the enamel rods appear hexagonal.

CROSS SECTION OF ENAMEL RODS

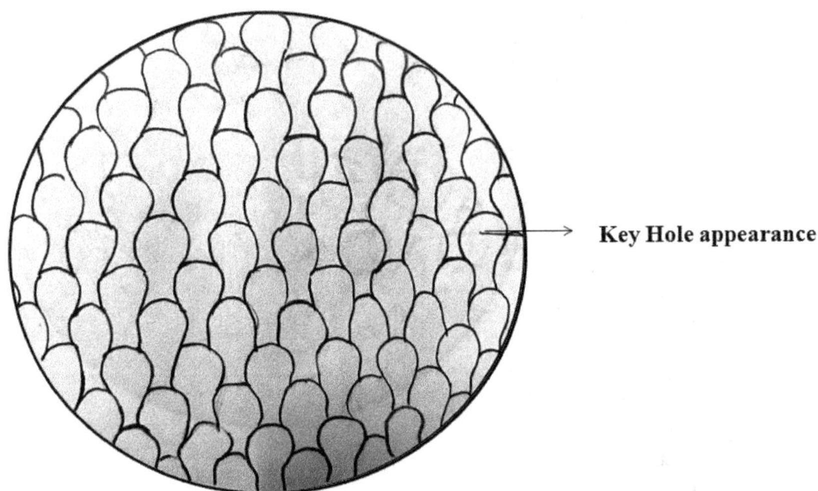

Human enamel seems to contain rods surrounded by rod sheaths and separated by interrod substance, a more common pattern is a key-hole or paddle-shaped prisms.

When cut longitudinally sections pass through the "heads" or "bodies" of one row of rods and the "tails" of an adjacent row. This produces an appearance of rods separated by interrod substance.

These rods measure about 5 μm in breadth and 9 μm in length. The bodies of the rods are nearer occlusal and incisal surfaces, whereas the tails point cervically.

INCREMENTAL LINES OF RETZIUS

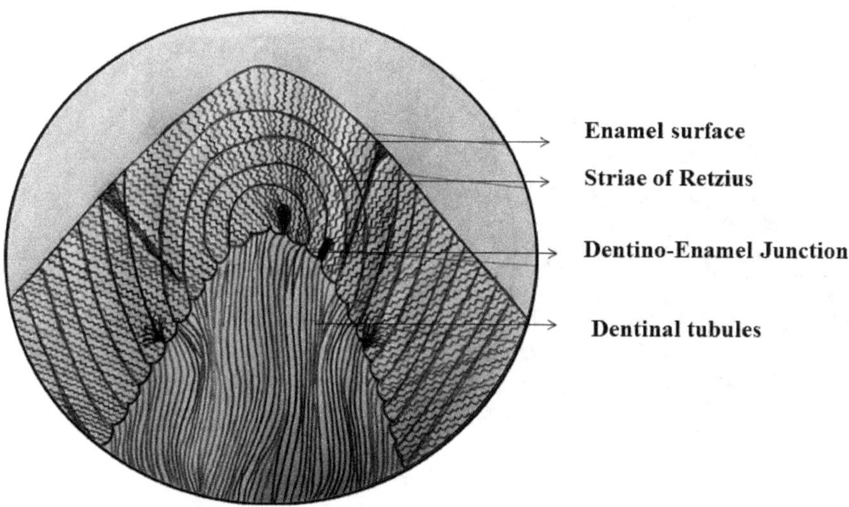

The Incremental lines of Retzius indicate the incremental or rhythmic deposition of enamel

These are seen as brownish lines that run obliquely across the enamel from dentino-enamel junction to the outer surface of enamel

The striae are wider apart in the middle portion of enamel while they are closer together and more numerous in the cervical enamel doe to slower deposition of enamel

In cross section these appear as concentric rings

The lines are less prominent in the enamel formed before birth and are more pronounced in the enamel formed after birth.

ENAMEL LAMELLAE

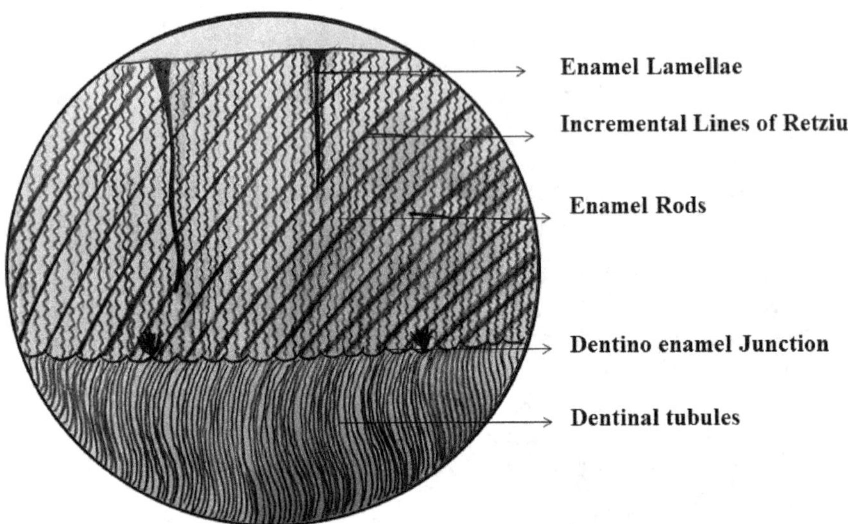

Enamel lamellae are leaf like structures extending from the outer surface of enamel towards the dentino-enamel junction.

These are formed due to severe disturbance causing a crack in the newly formed enamel and are filled with organic matter.

It is suggested that an enamel lamellae can be a weak site, providing a pathway for bacteria to enter and cause caries.

Enamel lamellae can be differentiated into three types.

Type A: Poorly calcified rod segments when a section of enamel fails to calcify

Type B: Contains only degenerated cells and the defects in enamel filled with organic material

Type C: Occurs in erupted teeth when the cracks are filled with organic m

ENAMEL TUFTS

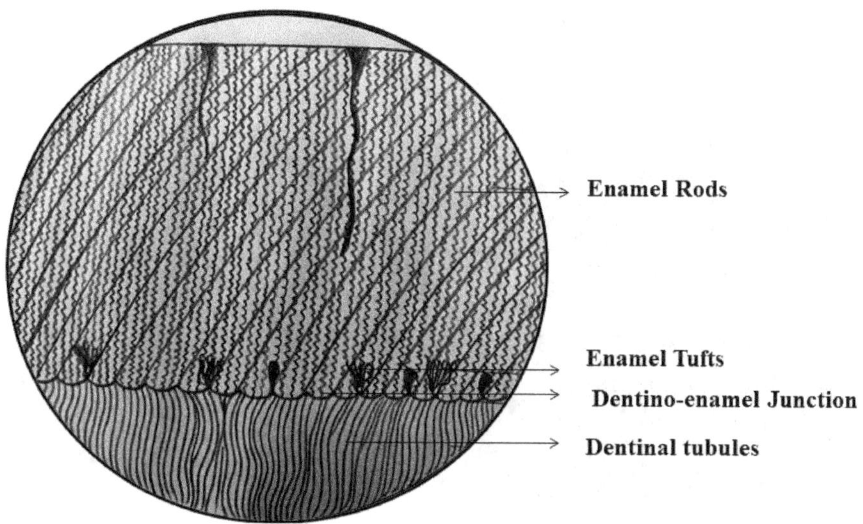

Enamel tufts are thin, wavy, ribbon like structures arising from the dentino enamel junction.

They reach to a short distance into the enamel, usually up to one third of the thickness.

When viewed under low magnification enamel tufts lying in different planes and curving in different directions are projected in one plane making them appear like a tuft of grass.

These structures are made up of hypocalcified enamel rods and have more organic component.

ENAMEL SPINDLES

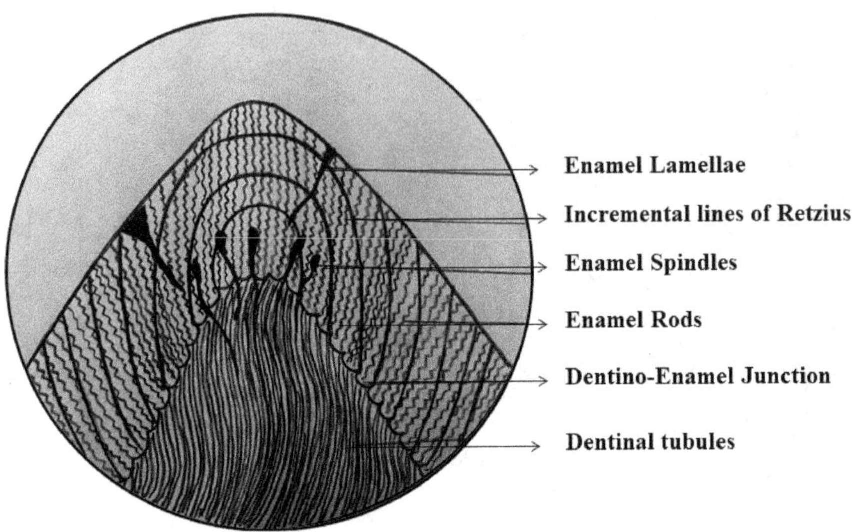

Enamel spindles are odontoblastic processes which pass across the dentino enamel junction into the enamel and become embedded in the enamel matrix

These are more abundant in the cuspal region

They presumably must have originated from those odontoblastic processes which had insinuated themselves between the cells of the inner enamel epithelium before either the dentin or the enamel was laid down.

The organic structure of spindle disintegrates and is replaced by air and thus enamel spindles appear as dark in transmitted light

GNARLED ENAMEL

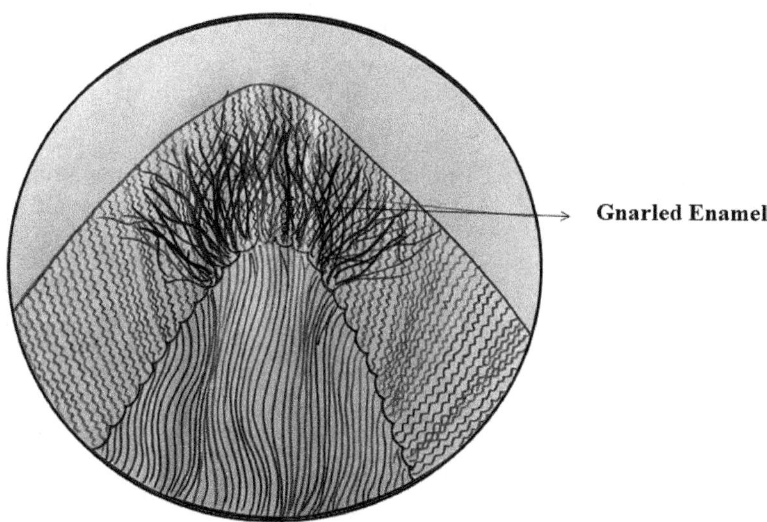

In some areas of enamel close to the dentino enamel junction, especially in the region of cusp, the wavy arrangement of the rods become marked, resulting in twisting of the rods.

These areas are called as gnarled enamel, which are associated with increased strength.

The enamel rods converge in the region of developmental pits and fissures on the occlusal surface of molars and premolars.

This change in the direction of rods is considered a functional adaptation that minimizes the risk of enamel fracture.

REFERENCES

1. Maji Jose. Manual of Oral Histology & Oral Pathology. Colour Atlas and Text. First edition.
2. Regezi, Sciubba and Jordan. Oral Pathology. Clinical pathologic correlations. Fifth edition.
3. R.Rajendran, B. Sivapathasundharam. Shafer's textbook of Oral Pathology -8th edition.
4. Brad. W. Neville, Douglas D. Damm, Carl M. Allen, Jerry E. Bouquot. Oral & Maxillofacial pathology. Elsevier publication. 2009; 3rd edition.
5. Shear and Paul M.Speight. Cysts of the Oral and Maxillofacial Regions. Fourth edition.
6. Peter A.Reichart and Hans P. Philipsen. Odontogenic tumours and allied lesions.

SLIDES ON ORAL PATHOLOGY AND ORAL HISTOLOGY - A COLOR ATLAS

Salient Features

This color atlas and text shows hand drawn histology and oral pathology diagrams

All the diagrams are drawn by the author herself.

Students of dentistry and clinicians will benefit from this book.

Useful for undergraduates, postgraduates, teaching faculties of oral pathology, oral medicine and the practitioners

R kalpana is working as Reader, Department of Oral Pathology and Oral Microbiology, RVS Dental College and Hospital. She has published several articles in various journals.

Dr. R.Kalpana
Reader
RVS Dental College & Hospital
Kannampalayam, Sulur-641402
Contact no- 9840307190
drkalpana86@gmail.com